ZAANAN

Episode Two: The Dream of Delosar

Written and Illustrated by

Al Bohl

© 1990 by Barbour and Company, Inc.
All Rights Reserved
Printed in the United States of America
ISBN 1-55748-124-5

Typesetting by:
Typetronix, Inc., Cape Coral, FL

A BARBOUR BOOK

TERMS AND PEOPLE YOU WILL READ ABOUT

Alien-thought - Any idea, religion, or movement contrary to Sphere.

Allison - Well-known artist of Sphere.

Asaph - Senior leader of a rebel space colony.

Baron - Military athlete and father of Zaanan.

Edolf - Leader of the terrorist Planetarians.

Holocaust - Nuclear world war in the twenty-fifth century.

Joseph - Zaanan's twin brother.

Kara - Medical research scientist and mother of Zaanan.

Malcolm - Head of Sphere's Secret Police (SSP).

Maroth - Absolute ruler of Troz.

Planetarians - A terrorist group desiring to overthrow the Sphere government.

Power arms - Pair of metallic gloves used for protection and complete communication by Talgents only; powered by nuclear fusion.

Sleep injection - A shot given that slows down body functions before a person is placed in a frozen state.

Sphere - One-world government of earth ruled by computer.

Stone, the - A minicomputer that looks like a rock. The computer contains the entire Bible and a concordance. It is activated by forming a fist around it and naming a subject or verse of Scripture. The user's skeleton is used as an amplifier to the user's eardrum.

Talgent - Highest rank earned by a military specialist who eliminates alien-thought.

Talgent Flara (Flame) - Female Talgent.

Thwart - Malcolm's bubbling assistant.

Troz - The largest of many rebel movements seeking world control over Sphere.

Zaanan (Zā′-năn) - A young military Talgent of the society of Sphere.

Space colony in the Fatal Limit

CHAPTER 1

Holocaust Year: A.D. 2453
Present Earth Year: A.D. 3007
Year of Sphere: 554
Location: Space colony in the Fatal Limit.

"Honor your father and your mother, so that you may live long in the land the Lord your God is giving you" (Exodus 20:12).

Wham! Jerous slammed his fist angrily onto the conference table. "Asaph, have you completely lost your mind?" he questioned with a mixed look of rage and bewilderment. "You say

1

you had a dream," he continued, "and you sent out a ship that brought back a Talgent warrior, a vowed enemy, into our once-hidden colony. We spent years developing the technology to sustain life in this nuclear waste dump. Years — carefully hiding our presence here from Sphere . . ."

"Jerous, Sphere and Troz know we're here, and you know that," said Joseph, looking for some way to defuse Jerous's verbal bombing.

"If they really knew we were here, they would have already attacked us," said Rufus.

Suddenly everyone in the room tried to express his opinion at once.

"Brothers," said Asaph in his soft-spoken manner.

Everyone at the table, including Jerous, silenced.

"Let Jerous continue," Asaph said. "You were saying we carefully hid our colony from Sphere."

Jerous adjusted his collar and began again, with less venom in his voice. "Asaph, how could you bring Talgent Zaanan here? How could you

2

Jerous's verbal bombing

show him everything, give him a Stone, and send him on his merry way? This very minute he is probably reporting everything to Sphere and preparing to come back here and destroy us."

After a long pause, the elderly Asaph slowly stood to his feet with the aid of Joseph. "Perhaps I was wrong," he began. "Maybe I should have ignored my dream, and yet as it turned out, someone was in need. How was I to know it would be a Talgent from Sphere?"

"Excuse me, sir, but what was your dream?" Rufus asked.

"Well, I dreamed about the story Jesus told of the farmer throwing seed. The seed fell in different soils: some on the road, some among thorns, some on rocks, and then some on good soil. Of course, seed couldn't sprout on the surface of a road; however, in my dream, that road was broken up and removed, and the soil underneath was ready for seed to grow in it.

"When I woke up, I felt that someone's heart — someone who once had been hardened to the

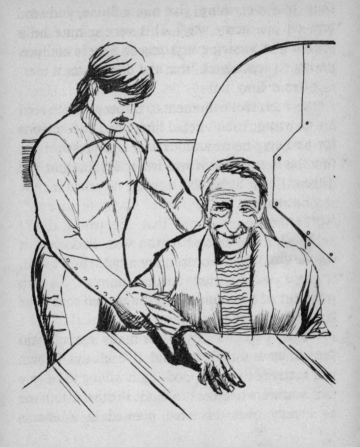

Asaph speaks

seed of God's Word — was now very ready. When I saw it was Zaanan, knowing his family history and knowing that Joseph here is his twin brother, I was certain that the dream was a message from God.

"So I seized the moment to throw as much seed his way as possible. I told him I had two reasons for believing he wouldn't reveal our presence. At first he seemed satisfied when I told him my dream. Later, as he was leaving, he asked me the second reason.

"To be honest, until that moment I didn't know what the second reason was. Suddenly, it was as if God put words in my mouth, and I said, 'I know your parents!' At that moment, his ship went out of communication range, and that's the last I've seen of him."

"Well, I've known you for many years," said Jerous, now satisfied, "and I've always known you to desire to please God. I am willing to believe that you were obedient to God. Brothers, join me as I pray over this seed planted in Zaanan's

"Joseph is Zaanan's twin brother"

heart."

Every man, even the elderly Asaph, got down flat on his face on the floor and prayed. Jerous voiced the prayer: "Our Father, King of the universe, in the name of Jesus I lift up Zaanan to You. I bind the power of Satan in his life and pray that the eyes of his heart would be open to the Gospel of Jesus Christ. We thank You that salvation is Your business, and we bind ourselves to Your will in this matter. Amen."

Where there had been strife, now there was unity as the men left the room. Jerous smiled at his old friend Asaph, who returned the expression. Now only Joseph remained with Asaph. The room was filled with silence for a long while. Joseph sat across from Asaph at the table, his chin resting on his folded arms.

"Dreams," said Asaph, finally breaking the quiet. "God speaks to us in dreams sometimes. God spoke to Joseph in the New Testament three times through dreams concerning the events surrounding the birth of Christ. He even spoke to the

"God speaks to us in dreams sometimes"

wise men in a dream. I don't believe that every dream is a message from the Almighty, or even most, but for certain some are."

Joseph patiently waited and listened as Asaph spoke. Asaph smiled as he looked at Joseph. "Your presence here is the result of a dream."

Joseph had heard the story before, but he didn't mind hearing it again and again.

"I was fifty-five," continued Asaph, "and it was time for me to be tested in Sphere to see if I could still function as a worthwhile citizen. Because of my Christian activities, I was certain I would fail the test, even if I actually passed it, so I left Sphere and went into hiding in a secluded area known as Delosar, a tropical rain forest perhaps as beautiful as the Garden of Eden.

"One day the Sphere military was having training exercises nearby. From a safe place I watched a young soldier climb the side of a mountain next to a waterfall. About halfway up, his vine broke, and he fell. No one else saw this, so I rescued him. He was badly hurt, so I nursed

10

Baron Falling

him back to health in my secret hiding place.

"As the days turned into weeks, we became good friends. I shared the Gospel with him, but he remained firm in his belief in the Sphere way. However, as loyal as he was to Sphere, he didn't turn me in.

"That young man was, of course, you and Zaanan's father. You boys really favor him. After his training, your father was selected to represent the Sphere military in athletic events. He won many contests and was a Sphere champion.

"As you know, when Sphere came to power as the one-world government, it abolished all marriage. The Sphere knew that people with families were harder to control. The Genetic Birth Division would use their computers to select a man and woman to mate and produce a certain child to fill a job for Sphere. Your father was selected to mate with a medical research scientist named Kara. They were to leave their jobs, go to Sphere's mountain resort area, and produce a

Champion of Sphere

child.''

"I don't understand why they had to go to a retreat area," Joseph said.

"Well, I suppose that Sphere found that people reproduced better in a relaxed setting," responded Asaph. "Anyway, Baron and Kara went to this mountain retreat. They were there for weeks.

"She became pregnant, and an early examination revealed that Kara would have twins. The Genetic Birth Division had ordered only one baby. Zaanan filled all the genetic requirements. Just a few weeks into Kara's pregnancy, you were marked in her womb. She was ordered to abort you by the third month of her pregnancy.

"Sphere had tried making machines out of people, without success. While at the retreat, Baron and Kara fell in love. After these early examinations, they were ordered to go back to their separate lives. Their last night together before leaving, Baron didn't sleep well. Finally he fell into a fitful sleep.

"Last night I dreamed of Delosar"

"The next morning Kara awoke to find Baron out on the balcony of their apartment. She went to him, and they embraced for a long time. Finally he said, 'Last night I dreamed of Delosar.'

"Naturally Kara didn't know what Delosar was. Baron had been awake since his dream, formulating a plan. They decided they would somehow fool the computer into showing that she had aborted you before the third month of her pregnancy, as ordered. Because Kara was a medical scientist, she found someone to help her conceal that she was still carrying twins.

"Baron requested that he be assigned to the Delosar area to get back in training. Though the Sphere forbade their seeing each other again, when possible, Kara and Baron stayed in contact — at much risk. When Kara was about to have the babies, she delivered you boys in seclusion.

"Baron took you and brought you to me, here in Delosar. Kara took Zaanan to the Sphere military nursery, where he was raised. I have kept you with me to this day. I'll never forget the

Meeting in Secret

mixture of love and hurt I saw in Baron's face as he held you for the last time. Before he left that day, we talked. Fighting back tears, Baron vowed that one day he would come back for you, bringing Kara and Zaanan with him. Somehow, someway, you would all live as a family.

"I asked him if he minded my praying that God would make it so. To my surprise, he allowed me to pray and even bowed his head. I haven't heard from Baron or Kara again personally. However, I have kept up with them when I could. In fact, I didn't know they were still alive until I told Zaanan they were. I know that they are both in their late fifties. With their brains and brawn, I'm certain they must have passed the sleep-injection test at least a few times."

Joseph's face was now buried in his folded arms. Asaph could hear his muffled sobs.

"In the Book of Acts, chapter ten, verse four, an angel came to a man named Cornelius in a dream. The angel said that his prayers had come up as a remembrance before God. I know that

"Somehow, someway we'll be together"

God the Father hasn't forgotten my prayer of long ago. Let's you and I pray together now, and let Him know we haven't forgotten. I believe that somehow, someway, you will all be together again.''

Joseph and Asaph held hands across the conference table and prayed earnestly.

Earnest Prayer

The Interrogation Room

At that very moment, as Asaph and Joseph prayed together, Zaanan was in a vastly different setting. He was thousands of miles away, back on earth in the interrogation offices of Sphere headquarters.

The room Zaanan sat in was small, with a large domed light above his head. The heat from the light, the tilt of his chair, and the extreme quiet made Zaanan uncomfortable. He had not been told why he was summoned, and he had waited there in that room for two hours all by himself.

This was all part of the Sphere's way of controlling people. People were left alone long enough to make them feel that Sphere had acquired some alien-thought information on them. People would nervously retrace their pasts as they waited, to have some sort of answer to any possible question that might arise.

The room was six feet wide on all four sides, with a twelve-foot-high ceiling.

Suddenly, without warning, a person's face covered the wall behind Zaanan. When the man first spoke, Zaanan nearly jumped out of his seat from surprise. His chair mechanically whipped around to face the ominous face. All this was done to make Zaanan more insecure.

"Zaanan, code number WD1-TR5-XD," began the face in rapid-fire wording, "are you nervous?"

"No," said Zaanan calmly (he hoped). A small orbed object made of polished metal entered the room and zipped around in the air, emitting a constant humming noise and frequent squeaks, sputters, and whistles. This six-inch ball added to the orchestra of fear in the Sphere room of interrogation. The ball would zoom close to

"Zaanan!"

Zaanan's head, even right up in his face. Zaanan felt an urge to reach up and swat the ball like an insect, but he resisted the impulse. The ball would then swoosh around behind him, only to pop up and squeal from time to time after one of his answers.

"We have reviewed your diary from the last week or so," said the face. "Do you swear the recorded events to be completely accurate, without flaw?"

"Yes," answered Zaanan.

The ball popped and wheezed.

"According to your diary, you left the Neo-Alpha I conference station as a decoy to lure the Troz guardian vessels away from a Troz messenger module. This is not a part of Sphere defense procedures. Why did you do this?"

"Irregular times call for irregular actions," Zaanan replied. "The messenger module was armed with Stingers."

"Stingers?"

"Yes, a new Troz defense projectile designed to attack an enemy's greatest heat source."

Pop, Squeal, Swoosh

"Did you know the module had Stingers on board before you attacked?"

"No."

"No?"

"Yes."

"Yes?"

"No, I mean whatever my diary says is correct. You're confusing me," charged Zaanan.

"Confusing?" pressed the face. "Do you often find the truth so confusing?"

"Listen, I was asleep. HB-Deen woke me . . ."

"HB-Deen? This is the computer you say was the controlling computer for the station? We have no records of any such computer in our system."

"Well, your records are wrong. Anyway, I was awakened, advised of the situation, and decided to lure the guardian vessels away so HB-Deen could retrieve the Troz messenger module. I didn't know the Stingers were on the messenger module. I defeated the Stingers, and my starjet was damaged. I floated in space until a Troz sentry ship and a space junker fought over me, at

"I decided to lure the guardian vessels away"

which time I evacuated in a jettison pod. I was picked up by a Sphere transport ship and returned to Neo-Alpha I.''

The ball squalled and whistled in a manner that seemed to show disbelief.

"Zaanan, code number WD1-TR5-XD," stated a different unseen person, "report to the assignment desk for new orders!"

"But I was checking Zaanan's diary!" pleaded the first interrogator.

"His diary checks out!" said the new voice.

"Listen, Zaanan has some real problems in his story that I need to ask him about."

"No, you listen to me. You mind-benders are all alike. You wouldn't know the truth if it slapped you in the face. Now let Talgent Zaanan, who happens to outrank you, go!"

A big smile erupted across Zaanan's face. Suddenly the table had turned, and Zaanan was in control. "Reporting, sir!" he said to his new faceless friend.

"Zaanan," said the face, "when you return, we will continue our diary probe. You're hiding

"Reporting, sir!"

something. I can feel it."

"You're paranoid," Zaanan retorted as he rose to his feet. The pesky ball whizzed right up into his face. Zaanan dodged, but the ball seemed to angrily challenge him.

"What's that behind you?" said Zaanan, pointing behind the face. The face turned, and Zaanan punched the ball with his fist as hard as he could. The little ball screamed as it bounced off three walls and the floor before rolling to a stop with a dull thud.

"What happened?" said the six-foot by twelve-foot face as it turned back toward Zaanan.

Zaanan shrugged his shoulders. "Wait and read my diary!"

Two walls parted at the corner, and Zaanan walked out, his knees shaking.

I don't know how much longer I could have answered questions, he thought to himself. *Why am I protecting those Christians? I could turn them in and say I was delaying in hopes of catching the leader. But Asaph said he knew my*

"KAAWHACK!"

parents, and I want to see them. He paused. *I would never see Allison again.*

Those two reasons seemed sufficient reason to keep his secret. He continued on to the next building for his assignment.

Allison

"Report to Malcolm"

CHAPTER 3

Zaanan made his way through the building and passed a maze of people busily working. Not one person spoke to him. That had never bothered him before, but now it did.

He flashed back in his mind to the cafeteria in the Fatal Limit. All those people, young and old, were talking, laughing, and hugging. The love he saw there had touched him more than he had realized.

Finally he found the assignment desk. The computer receptionist instructed him to report to Malcolm promptly at the SSP (Sphere Secret Police).

That's not what I wanted to hear, thought Zaanan. This meant that he had to go to the other side of the city of Sphere to see Malcolm. It was two o'clock, which meant a city shift change. Most people in Sphere had two separate jobs. Their first job started at eight o'clock in the morning and ended in time for them to diary their morning's activities and get to their next job, which lasted until eight at night. This shift change was a mad dash from one location to another. Zaanan knew that Malcolm had timed it to place him in the thick of this confusion. Finally Zaanan arrived at Malcolm's office.

"What kept you?" poked Malcolm as Zaanan entered his office. "I put in an assignment request for you hours ago."

Zaanan didn't bother to answer as he sat down across the desk from Malcolm, who was visibly pleased to see that he had annoyed Zaanan.

"What do you want?" Zaanan asked.

"Have you ever been to the Sleep Center?" toyed Malcolm.

Sphere City Shift Change

"No, I haven't."

"Well, today is your day. Or should I say *night?*"

"Get to the point, Malcolm!" flashed Zaanan.

"Well, it seems that a terrorist group called the Planetarians are supposed to break into the Sleep Center tonight and take a few bodies. We want you to be there to help capture this group and protect our little dreamland."

At age fifty-five, all citizens of Sphere were tested physically and mentally. If they failed the test, they were given a sleep injection and later placed in a frozen state. As younger people became ill and needed certain body organs, the parts would be taken from the frozen people, who were kept frozen for only thirty years.

"Meet us at midnight at the underground entrance on the north side of the Sleep Center. Oh, Zaanan — be sure your power arms are charged up and you have plenty of Hydrocaps," Malcolm added.

"Well, today is your day."

A few minutes before midnight, Zaanan arrived at the north entrance to the Sleep Center. This entrance was about fifty yards from the actual facility. He was the only one there.

I must be a little early — or a little late, he thought to himself. The latter idea made him grimace because he knew that being late would give Malcolm something else to tease him about.

He didn't have long to wait before he began to hear the echo of laser blasts and explosions coming from down inside the tunnel entrance.

"Well, it doesn't look like they waited for me," he muttered as he plunged into the entrance. The entrance itself was an underground tunnel large enough to drive a vehicle through. Zaanan didn't know that this entrance even existed, so apparently it was chosen in hopes of surprising the Planetarians. From the sound of things, it appeared that the Planetarians didn't appreciate surprises.

As Zaanan neared the end of the tunnel, a Sphere Secret Policeman burst through the door.

The Sleep Center

He rolled and tried to get to his feet, but his leg was hurt. Zaanan ran up to him. Just as he got to him and started to pick him up, an explosion hit the doorway, knocking both Zaanan and the man to the floor.

"These guys are playing for keeps," Zaanan said as he got to his feet. He pulled the policeman aside. "What can you tell me?" he asked the man hurriedly.

"There were ten of us and Malcolm," the man answered between breaths and waves of pain. "Malcolm felt we needed to go on in. We didn't know that there were so many of them or that they had so many weapons."

"How many are there?"

The policeman slumped back without answering. Zaanan checked his pulse. He was still alive, just unconscious. Another explosion nearby lit up the darkness, spewing concrete, sparks, and smoke everywhere.

Zaanan rushed in and darted around the

An explosion hits the doorway

corner. The giant dome was not well-lighted. The frequent explosions added light to some areas.

Zaanan felt his way over to some long plastic tubes that appeared to be about three feet in diameter. An explosion hitting on the other side of the tube lit up the tube. Zaanan looked up, but he wasn't ready for what he saw. In that flash of light, Zaanan saw that a man was lying flat in the tube. He appeared to be asleep. He was slowly rotating on a cushion of fog or smoke that mostly concealed his image. Zaanan knew these people had been given the sleep injection and many were already frozen, but he had never pictured what this place looked like.

For a moment he stepped back and tried to get a different view of the Sleep Center. The tubes were about six and one-half feet long, capped on each end. Tubes had been placed in a row, end to end, as far as he could see in either direction. Like bunk beds, the long row of tubes had tiers of tubes stacked on top of them all the way to the ceiling.

A Sleep Tube

Zaanan couldn't get over how young and healthy the frozen man looked. He had never thought of the age of fifty-five as anything but old, but possibly this man was not fifty-five. Maybe he had been contaminated with alien-thought, and this was his punishment.

Sphere sure doesn't play games, he thought.

"Zaanan! Look out!" a voice screamed in the dark.

He jumped just as a laser blast hit where he had stood. He slid under the tubes to the other side, which as it turned out, was only an aisle between rows of tubes.

"This place is creepy!" he said out loud.

"It sure is!" replied Malcolm as he leaped to cover beside Zaanan.

"What happened?" Zaanan asked.

"Our source said the Planetarians planned to arrive at midnight, at the north entrance. We were going to head them off. They beat us in here and were ready for us," Malcolm admitted.

"How many are in here?"

Malcolm leaps beside Zaanan

"I'm not sure, but judging from their firepower, the place must be crawling with them."

"Where are our people?"

"I don't know!"

"I'm going to see if I can locate any of them. Tune to frequency *M*."

Zaanan looked around and stepped back. Next he looked up to the roof of the dome. He set his power arms to "flight mode" and raised his hands toward the roof. The power arms propelled him a hundred feet straight up, past tier after tier of sleeping people.

When he reached the top level, he landed on a metal catwalk that ran along both sides of the tubes. A laser blast whizzed past his head, just barely missing him. He fell flat on the catwalk, then turned over on his back as another blast hit the ceiling of the dome.

As his eyes adjusted from the blast of the laser light, he saw a small cluster of mirrors attached to the ceiling. Another blast bounced off one of

Flight Mode

the mirrors, angling in a new direction. Zaanan slowly stood to his feet as another blast approached. He watched the line of fire and followed where it reflected to another mirror on the perimeter of the dome before striking below. He turned around and saw little mirrors all around the perimeter of the dome. All the laser blasts seemed to be coming from the same place.

He quickly switched his power arms to "heat sensory mode" and pointed in the direction of the laser. His power arms showed 98.7 degrees at the southeast portion of the dome.

"Wow!" he exclaimed. "It must be just one person firing that laser. He must be using heat sensory to pinpoint our position.

"Malcolm," he whispered into his power arm communication system.

"Yes," came the reply.

"There is only one person firing that laser gun."

"What?"

"That's right. He has mirrors positioned all

Heat Sensory Mode

over the place, and he uses heat sensory to find us."

"He must be running interference for another group somewhere in the dome," deducted Malcolm."

"Do you want me to take him out now?" Zaanan asked.

"No. Record a visual of his laser and find the others first. We need to know about their technology in case we somehow miss them."

"Okay. Here I go."

Zaanan ran down the catwalk toward the south end of the dome. Using his power arms, he flew from aisle to aisle until he was above the laser gun.

"Malcolm, I was right. It's one guy. I'm recording now."

"Good. Now find some other warm bodies," ordered Malcolm.

The Planetarian continued to hold the police at bay with frequent laser blasts. Malcolm ordered everyone to stay put. Using his heat

Flying from aisle to aisle

sensors Zaanan scanned the dome for more Planetarians and located two groups at opposite ends of the dome on the ground level.

"Malcolm, I see two groups of two each. One is near me, about four aisles over," Zaanan reported.

"Get a visual for us," Malcolm commanded. "And a location."

"All right. There is a group on the extreme west section of the dome, on aisle twenty-one. Also, the group nearer me is on the east end, on aisle thirty-six. I'll bounce over and get a visual."

Malcolm ordered the remaining six officers to split up and head for aisles twenty-one and thirty-six. This was difficult to do between laser blasts. Zaanan flew over to the catwalk on aisle thirty-six. He was shocked at what he saw.

"Malcolm," he reported, "you won't believe this. The Planetarians have taken three of the sleep tubes, stacked them in a triangle, and saddled them together. There is a driver on top and a

Splitting Up

blaster mounted on back. Rockets run down both sides. They've turned the sleep tubes into a space ship! They're going to ride them out of here. These people know what they're doing. Are your people in position?''

"I hope so!''

Suddenly the laser gun went wild, firing in all directions.

"They're moving!'' Zaanan screamed.

Phtoom!

A laser blast exploded next to Zaanan, then another and another. He fell to the catwalk on his knees. *He must have found me. I'd better get out of here!*

He stood to run, only to be cut off by a laser blast. He turned, and another blast stopped him. Then one hit the catwalk at his feet. Zaanan fell through the catwalk. Using the "power grip" mode in his power arms, he locked onto the rim of the catwalk. The power grip locked the fingers of the gloves into a grip that was impossible to break.

"They found me!"

The two Planetarians looked up and saw him, then jumped onto their makeshift tubeship. One was driving; the other faced the back with a laser blaster. Their rockets roared to life. Zaanan was dangling by one arm near the roof of the dome a hundred feet up.

"Stun mode," he said, voice activating his free power arm. Then he fired an electrical shock at the tubeship, hitting the driver, who slumped over just as the craft began to move. The Planetarian laser gunman fired on Zaanan again.

"Why didn't I think of this before?" Zaanan exclaimed, barking "quake mode" at his power arm. He pointed in the area of the cluster of mirrors on the ceiling, and the sonic waves blew them to pieces.

"Malcolm, I took out the laser gun. Get him."

"We're moving!"

The gunman on the back of the tubeship below Zaanan jumped into the driver's seat and started to fly off.

"Stun mode!" shouted Zaanan.

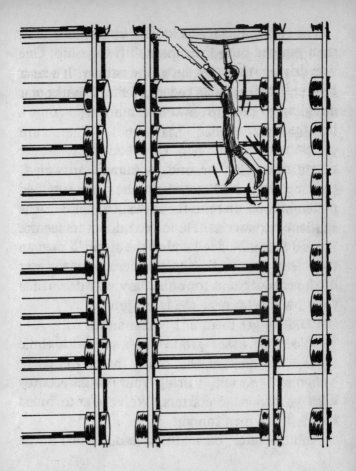

Quake Mode

I've got to lead him just a little, he thought as the tubeship picked up speed.

Tis-year! fired Zaanan's power arm. It was a direct hit. The man jerked and fell off. Without a driver, the tubeship slowed to a hover.

"Zaanan!" yelled Malcolm. "Where are you?"

"Just hanging around," Zaanan answered, swaying a hundred feet above the pavement. He pulled himself up onto the catwalk again. He was suddenly exhausted. He looked down to see the Sphere Secret Police helping the stunned men to their feet, then walked to the elevator at the end of the catwalk and took the easy way down. He found Malcolm near the laser gun.

"Did we get them all?" Zaanan asked.

"No. The other group got away with three tubes. We did get the other three, though," Malcolm reported. "Bring your visual records with you to headquarters. We've got to interrogate these men tonight."

An hour later, back at the headquarters of the

Suddenly exhausted

Sphere Secret Police, Malcolm and his aides were preparing to question the captives, who were to be strapped to a table with metal bands wrapped around their foreheads. Zaanan dropped his visual records by the evidence desk and went to the interrogation room.

"Zaanan, come in," said Malcolm, with no barbs in his voice. "Have you seen our new technology?"

"No, I haven't," the Talgent answered.

"We can now extract all the thoughts from a person's mind and even tap his subconscious. Of course, the person isn't much good after that. We've sent in a report to the Judicial Sphere computer and are waiting for permission to probe. Then we will give them the sleep injection for alien-thought activities and freeze them," Malcolm explained.

"Tonight?" Zaanan asked.

"Alien-thought is a virus. Time isn't on our side. It must be dealt with before others are infected."

"Have you seen our new technology?"

PERMISSION GRANTED flashed the judicial computer monitor.

"If you're finished with me, I think I'll go and get some rest," Zaanan said.

"I don't think so, Za. We need to retrieve the missing Sleep Center tubes. I'm sure the Sphere will assign you to the case. You need to know this information firsthand," Malcolm continued. "You also need to see how deadly alien-thought can be." Malcolm stared deeply into Zaanan's eyes, as if to say that Zaanan was under suspicion.

Zaanan was suddenly sure that Thwart, Malcolm's assistant, had reported that Zaanan had helped some Christians escape the other night.

Malcolm and Zaanan stood in a booth behind tinted glass as workers strapped the captives down. Not one captive resisted, as if it were some sort of honor to die for their cause. As each was probed, injected, and frozen, Zaanan stood motionless thinking how insensitive and cruel it all was.

"Alien-thought can be deadly"

But Malcolm seemed to enjoy himself. At the conclusion, Zaanan started to leave.

"You don't look too well, old friend," poked Malcolm. "We got the information you need from them. Be happy."

Zaanan didn't speak. He couldn't. He just left. He could hear Malcolm laughing behind him, and the laughter rang in his ears as he walked out into the early morning.

The city of Sphere hadn't yet awakened from its night of slumber. Zaanan saw a little sparrow hopping along, pecking at the ground for insects. The sun began to come up, chasing the night away again. Suddenly his life seemed pointless — empty. He felt sick to his stomach. Thoughts of right and wrong raced through his mind as he mechanically made his way back to his living quarters and went to sleep.

Although he had slept for four hours, it felt more like four minutes when the call came in on his audiovisual computer.

"Zaanan. Zaanan," said the assignment desk computer from headquarters.

Dawn

Zaanan rolled out of bed, pulled on a robe, and walked into the next room, where the unit was. "Yes? This is Zaanan," he reported in a groggy voice.

"Report to the assignment desk."

"I was up all night on assignment. Can I come in later?"

"Report to the assignment desk."

"Listen. Just punch in my assignment, and I'll get to it in a couple of hours. It would take me a couple of hours to get to headquarters, anyway."

"Report to the assignment desk," the receptionist repeated, not wavering or changing its monotone voice.

"Wait a min —" Zaanan started to say, his voice reflecting anger. But it was too late: The transmission was over. He stood leaning over his computer desk, staring a moment at the screen. He ran his lefthand fingers through his hair, pushing it back off his forehead, and then rubbed his face with both hands, trying to wake himself up.

His muscles were extremely sore, especially the shoulder he had hung from for so long the night

"Report to the assignment desk"

before. The pain went into his neck, giving him a headache.

Within two hours, he was at the assignment desk waiting for orders. He was wide-awake, in full uniform, and ready to go. As he suspected, he was to bring back the bodies that had been stolen from the Sleep Center and eliminate the alien-thought of the Planetarians. He programmed all the available data about the group into the memory banks of his power arms' computer. His orders were to leave within the hour.

He'd hoped to see Allison for a while before leaving. He had some questions for her about the Christian view of right and wrong. He tried to convince himself that this was his sole motive; however, in his heart he knew he just wanted to be near her again.

He also had some thoughts about the night before that he needed to report to Malcolm. Rather than fight the city shift change again, he opted to use the Vision-Phone. The computer receptionist answered and said that Malcolm was unable to come to the phone.

Vision-Phone

"Where is he, asleep?" Zaanan said jealously.

"No, he was requested by the Genetic Birth Division for reproduction assignment," the computer answered.

"Oh, I see. Well, prepare to record my transmission and see that he gets this as soon as possible."

"Yes, sir. I'm recording," assured the computer.

"Malcolm," Zaanan began, "I've had some thoughts about last evening I wanted to tell you about before I left. First of all, I feel that it had to be an inside job. The Planetarians didn't arrive just before us and install all those laser mirrors. It took weeks of planning and a full knowledge of where everything is in the dome. I also feel that the people taken weren't randomly selected. Each one was chosen for a reason. Check out all employees from the top to the bottom. Transmission complete."

Zaanan left Sphere headquarters and headed for his new assignment.

"I've had some thoughts about last evening"

Final check

Malcolm was very excited as he arrived at the Center for Genetic Science. The male and female selected to have a baby were checked out one final time before meeting in person. Malcolm entered a small room with black walls all around. Only a lone lighted disc in the center of the room was visible. He stepped onto the lighted disc on the floor and nine four-inch by six-inch rectangular columns began to rise to just above his waist, forming a circle around him. Shafts of lights radiated up from each column.

Malcolm placed his hands on top of the columns in front of him. After a moment, the columns retreated and the wall to his left began to rise, revealing his mate.

"Surprised?" Malcolm asked as he came into full view of his mate.

"Not really," answered Allison.

"I thought for sure you would be," Malcolm said as he walked over to her.

"You must have done something to the computer."

"Allison, you surprise me! I think we make a perfect match."

"So you did alter the computer."

He walked over to her and tried to kiss her, but she turned her face and walked away before he could.

"Are you rejecting me?" he inquired. "One of the most powerful men in Sphere! Is it because you have found another one to fill your heart? Could it be one named Zaanan?"

She remained with her back to him. He walked over behind her and spoke into her right ear. "I'm sure you know that love is forbidden in Sphere and choosing your own mate is considered alien-thought. Do you want me to

"Love is forbidden"

describe in detail what would happen to both people accused of something of this nature?"

Allison didn't flinch.

"Well, then, let me tell you," Malcolm continued. "First they take the man . . ."

Allison swung around and tried to slap Malcolm in the face. He caught her hand and squeezed her wrist until it hurt.

"Sphere knows what you're doing here," Allison said. "It's all being recorded."

Malcolm relaxed his hold and began to laugh. "Allison, I'm head of Sphere's Secret Police. Do you think I would be stupid enough to talk openly in a room if I weren't sure it was safe? I've checked this area out. We are all alone."

"It's Zaanan you really want to punish, isn't it?" reasoned Allison. "You want to trap him in alien-thought to get rid of him."

Malcolm was now the silent one, so she continued. "He told me how you were best friends at the academy and how your friendship turned to hate when he received the Talgent position instead of you."

Trying to slap Malcolm

"I deserved it! He didn't!" Malcolm screamed.

"In case someone is listening, Zaanan is my friend, and that's all," Allison pleaded.

Malcolm grabbed her by both shoulders and pulled her close. "I have a special place for you in my prison where you can wait for your hero to come. When he hears — and I'll make sure he does — he will come for you, and I'll be ready for him. I'll show you both the poisonous bite of alien-thought."

"Your bitterness has driven you mad!" Allison screamed.

Malcolm pulled his stun gun and fired it at her. When she collapsed to the floor, he picked her up and carried her out of the Center for Genetic Science.

"Did you get it all?"

"Yes, Dr. Kara, I recorded their every word. I assume Malcolm is unaware of our new bugging system?"

Stunned

"Yes, it seems he is. Of course, that is just what we wanted. This is more proof that Malcolm has been toying with the Sphere computer system," Kara said.

"What is he doing?" her helper asked.

"We feel he has been arranging the unrequired matching of people to produce infants that he then sells on the black market," Kara replied. "He's clever, but we're getting closer to catching him."

"What do I do with this tape?"

"Give it to me. I'll put it in a safe place."

Kara left the security area and went to her office. She sat in her chair with the lights off while she began to formulate a plan to catch Malcolm and at the same time save her son Zaanan's life. She had seen Zaanan from a distance many times and was proud of his accomplishments. She didn't dare approach him; contact between parents and children was against the law of Sphere. Once she had given birth to him, he belonged to Sphere, not her. She had not heard from him since the night he was born. As she

"I'll put this tape in a safe place"

pictured her son in her mind, tears began to flow down her cheeks, around the corners of her mouth, and onto her lab coat. She didn't brush them away, feeling they helped cleanse her mind of the hurt.

Tears of cleansing

Malcolm's carcopter landing

Allison lay motionless in the back of Malcolm's carcopter as he arrived on the roof of the headquarters of the Secret Police. Rain was pelting down hard in big drops.

"Allison?" he called.

Allison was still under the effects of the electrical shock from his stun gun. He gently tugged her left arm at the elbow to see if she would respond, then looked out at the rain coming down in sheets.

I'll go get Thwart to help me move her, he thought. He jumped out of his carcopter and dashed for the door to the building, running as if the rain would melt him.

Since the Holocaust some five hundred years earlier, the earth's weather had been very strange and unpredictable. Any weather was possible any time. Snow was not uncommon in the summer in areas where it had once been very uncommon. Rain and drought could be even more extreme in portions of the world where monsoons should have been unlikely. Dry spells plagued tropical forests and deserts were sometimes flooded.

Birds, animals, and insects had a terrible time adjusting to their changing environments. Plant life suffered even more. So many plants died that erosion destroyed much of the top soil and not enough oxygen was produced. Sphere had a colossal job on its hands in developing new ways to produce food and oxygen.

Even the salt and nutritional resources of the oceans were seriously damaged. Man's desire to control the destiny of the world at the time of the nuclear Holocaust only served to lessen his control.

Relentless rain

Allison began to recover from the electric shock. Her jaw hurt from clenching her teeth; her fingers and toes felt numb. She realized she was in Malcolm's carcopter somewhere in the rain.

"Where am I?" she wondered. *"And where's Malcolm?"* The fact that he wasn't there was enough to make her rejoice. She sat up, and her head pounded. Her coordination was impaired but returning slowly. She pulled herself into the front seat and unlatched the door. The wind blew cold rain in on her. She pushed the door open and fell out onto the roof; her legs were still numb. The blinding rain made it difficult for her to see where she was.

"There's a door!" she exclaimed, seeing a door on a small house on top of the roof. She tried the door, but it was locked. Her strength was now returning, and she walked over to the edge of the roof and looked down seventy-two stories to the street.

Suddenly, above the storm, she heard the door

Seventy-two stories down to the street

opening. Thwart and an assistant came into view.

"Would you look at this rain!" Thwart complained. "Did you know it was raining?"

"No," replied the assistant.

Allison stood leaning as close as possible to the outside wall of the small house.

"Make sure that door doesn't lock behind us!" Thwart yelled, trying to be heard above the storm.

"Okay!"

"Let's get the girl and get back in fast."

Thwart and his helper started for Malcolm's carcopter, and Allison seized the moment to slip inside the door. A set of stairs led to an elevator. She ran down the stairs and pressed the elevator call button.

Wait a minute! she thought as her mind cleared. *If I go in there all wet, I'll be easy to spot.* She knew it wouldn't be but a moment before Thwart realized she had escaped.

"Let's get the girl!"

The elevator door opened. Allison stepped in and let water drip from her clothes, then jumped back out. She ran over to a dark corner and curled herself into a ball to hide.

Just as the elevator door closed, Thwart and his assistant burst in. Allison breathed as shallowly as possible, trying to become invisible as Thwart pressed the elevator call button and slammed his fist into the closed door.

"We missed her!" he cried.

His helper punched him on the shoulder and pointed to a trail of water that led into Allison's shadowed corner.

"You may as well give up," Thwart exclaimed. "There's nowhere to hide."

Allison slowly stood to her feet, walked out of the shadows, and went with them without incident to a secluded area of the building.

"This is Malcolm's private little prison," said Thwart. "In fact, only a few of us even know this place exists. Isn't that right, Leo?"

"Right, Thwart."

"We missed her!"

"Leo, here, is your jailer. He'll get you some new clothes and food. We want to make your visit as pleasant as possible. Right, Leo?"

"That's right, Thwart." Both men laughed and turned to go.

Allison looked about her cell. No windows, no color — just four padded walls, a cot, toilet, and a single light panel in the ceiling. She knew her every move was being monitored by camera. This was all an elaborate trap for Zaanan.

She sat down on the edge of her cot, cold from her rain-drenched clothing. She hadn't been searched at all, so she still had her Stone in her pocket. Hiding her actions the best she could, she made a fist around the small computer that looked like a rock and said, "trials."

The Stone searched through its concordance and began quoting Scripture, using her skeleton as an amplifier to her eardrums.

"James one, verses two to four," said the Stone. "Consider it pure joy, my brothers, whenever you face trials of many kinds, because

"Trials"

you know that the testing of your faith develops perseverance. Perseverance must finish its work so that you may be mature, complete, not lacking anything.

"First Peter one, verses six and seven: In this you greatly rejoice, though now for a little while you may have had to suffer grief in all kinds of trials. These have come so that your faith — of greater worth than gold, which perishes even though refined by fire — may be proved genuine and may result in praise, glory and honor when Jesus Christ is revealed."

"Strength," Allison whispered.

"Psalms twenty-seven, verse one: The Lord is my light and my salvation, whom shall I fear? The Lord is the stronghold of my life — of whom shall I be afraid?

"Second Chronicles sixteen, verse nine: For the eyes of the Lord range throughout the earth to strengthen those whose hearts are fully committed to him.

"Proverbs eighteen, verse ten: The name of

"Strength"

the Lord is a strong tower; the righteous run to it and hide.''

Allison opened her fist as she felt her entire body relax. She thought of the words to an ancient hymn she had recently learned. The song was called ''Whispering Hope,'' and the words said:

> ''Will not the deepening darkness,
> Brighten the glimmering stars?''

Her situation hadn't changed, but Allison had. ''Heavenly Father,'' she mouthed silently, ''I don't see how this will work out, but my trust, my hope, is in You. Even if I die, I will praise You. Please use all this for Your glory and to the salvation of Zaanan. Forgive me for being angry at Malcolm. Loose Malcolm and Zaanan from their bitterness. I also pray that Malcolm will come to know You. Your Word says to thank You in every situation, so I thank You now. In Jesus' name I pray, amen.''

Praying

She lay back on her cot and tried to warm herself, but to no avail.

In a few hours, she was awakened by her cell door opening. Leo brought her a blanket, some prison clothing, a towel, and food.

"Thank you, Leo," Allison said.

Leo didn't say a word. He looked around the cell at the ceiling and then back to the door. Allison was separating the items on her cot. As Leo left, he knocked on the door softly to get her attention and then walked out. As the door closed, Allison looked up. Leo had drawn a small frown on the door.

Allison smiled, walked over to the door, and drew a line resembling a smile under the frown with her finger, symbolically completing the shape of a fish.

Leo is an underground Christian! she rejoiced to herself.

Through the centuries, and even then, the fish

Leo knocking softly

was a Christian symbol. One person would draw a frown, and the other would finish the drawing of the fish. To a nonbeliever, the frown would mean nothing.

Leo did nothing unusual at work that day. When his shift was over, he recorded his diary and left for his living quarters. Since it was eight at night, his second shift was over, and he was free.

Leo left Sphere Secret Police headquarters and walked several blocks to the city of Sphere's underground transportation system. There he waited for his train. When it came, he got on and rode three stops before he got off. The platform was filled with waiting people. He strode over to a wall near a tunnel and leaned against it.

In a few minutes, a train pulled in going the opposite direction on the track on the other side of the platform. As the people pushed into the train, Leo simply jumped onto the empty track beside him. He crouched down and peeked to see if anyone saw him, then he crawfished backward

Peeking

and started to walk down the track, deeper into the tunnel.

Coming to a boarded-up door that opened to the inside, he squeezed in and closed the door behind himself. That door was the boundary between two distinct worlds. The side he came from was new, polished, and well-kept. The side he went to was ancient, dirty, and crumbling.

Sphere built the new transportation system right on top of the rubble of the world war. Collapsed walls, broken train tracks, and cracked foundations bore witness to the tragic past.

Leo carefully made his way down the abandoned train tunnel, occasionally looking back to make sure he was alone. Choking dust fell on him as the modern trains roared by above him. He always braced himself until they passed, never sure that something else wasn't about to fall around him.

As the tunnel deepened, he took out a light. The tunnel opened to an old platform area. As he

Leo walking down the old tunnel

walked along, he saw some writing on a crumbling bench. He tried to rub off the dust and dirt, but the bench crumbled in his hands. He could faintly make out the words "St. Louis Transportation System."

S-T Louis? he said to himself. *I wonder what the S-T stood for?*

At the end of the platform he took some stairs down three levels, went into another abandoned tunnel, and entered another boarded-up door.

"Hello, Brother Leo!" said a man who appeared to be more of a greeter than a guard.

"Hi, Tidwell," Leo answered. "I need to get a message to Asaph."

"Sure. Come in." He walked along beside Leo.

"The rumble is getting worse down here," Leo observed.

"Yes, it is. We have three shifts working, just to keep this place propped up. You should be here tomorrow, when the Sphere holiday season begins."

deeper and deeper and deeper

"Really?"

"They'll run more trains on tighter schedules, which means more vibrations and more collapsing down here," Tidwell explained as they passed a work crew working on a water leak.

"Makes you not want to ride the train, doesn't it?" Leo asked.

"One of these days, this whole place is going to go," agreed Tidwell as they entered the control area.

Leo walked on without Tidwell into the communication area of the abandoned subway system. The underground communication center was relatively small to serve as the link between all the Christian outposts. Stacks of television monitors with exposed wiring filled much of the area. Five people made up the communication team. They busily worked on bizarre equipment that was beyond verbal description.

"I need to speak with Asaph in the Limit," Leo explained to the communication officer.

Underground communication center

"Well, hello Leo. Sure. Have a seat."

In a few minutes Asaph's face filled a large screen in front of Leo.

"It's good to hear from you, Leo. How are you feeling?" Asaph asked.

"Fine, sir. My reason for calling is that Malcolm, my superior, has placed Allison in jail."

"In jail?"

"Yes, sir. Malcolm's assistant, Thwart, told me that Malcolm and Allison were selected as mates by the Genetic computer. Thwart feels that Malcolm is really trying to get at Talgent Zaanan. He seems to feel that Zaanan and Allison have feelings for each other."

"Thank you, Leo," said Asaph. "Can you give me any information as to her location?"

"Yes, sir. I can send a diagram of the building, her location, work schedules, and things like that."

"Wonderful! Thank you for your help. We'll be in contact with you."

Calling Asaph

"Yes, sir," Leo replied.

In the Limit, Asaph turned around in his chair, debating about whether or not to tell Joseph of Allison's situation. He knew how deeply Joseph loved Allison.

Joseph had desired to marry her for several years, but she wanted to pursue her art interests before starting a family. She was several years younger than Joseph. Asaph feared that telling him might force him to do something foolish.

"Yes, sir?" Joseph said as he entered Asaph's study. "I came as soon as I received your message."

"Joseph, there's something I need to tell you about Allison."

Immediately Asaph had Joseph's attention. "What is it? Is there a problem?"

"She has been taken by the Sphere Secret Police and is being held in a special prison section of the building."

"Allison has been taken by the SSP"

"Why? What's the reason?"

"They feel that Allison and Zaanan are romantically involved, and they are trying to trap your brother into rescuing her. This would give them enough evidence to convict him of alien-thought."

"Is it true?"

"I don't know, son. Allison was assigned by me to contact Zaanan and talk with him more about Christ. This could have easily been misunderstood by the SSP."

"Where is Zaanan?"

"Our sources say he's away from Sphere on assignment. There's one more thing, Joseph. The Genetic Birth Division of Sphere has assigned Allison to have a child with Malcolm."

"Malcolm! The head of the Sphere Secret Police? I've got to go to her and help her!"

"Joseph, we have plenty of qualified people in the city of Sphere to handle this. Besides, no one there knows that you even exist. You don't know

"I've got to go to her"

your way around Sphere; you've been sheltered from all that," pleaded Asaph.

"I can't just sit here. I must *do* something!" yelled Joseph, striking his fist on the conference table.

Asaph leaned forward to grab Joseph's hand. "You would just get in the way. It's not humanly possible for you to rescue her. I'm sorry, Joseph, but I must forbid you from going to Sphere."

Joseph slowly stood and left without saying a word.

Asaph sat back in his chair, slowly exhaled, and began to pray and plan. An hour later, he pulled himself up and got in his air-walker. He made his way through the corridors of their space colony, heading for dinner in the cafeteria.

On the way, he decided to see if Joseph was ready to eat. Perhaps he could cheer him up. Asaph felt he might have been too harsh on the young man. When he reached Joseph's quarters, no one was in, but Mark, a good friend of

"I must do something!"

Joseph's, was walking by.

"Have you seen Joseph?" Asaph inquired of the young man.

"Yes, sir. I watched his ship leave the departure bay about forty-five minutes ago," Mark replied.

"Did he say where he was going?"

"No, sir. He just left. Are you all right?"

"Yes, son, I'm fine," Asaph said as he turned around to head back toward his study.

"You know, it's funny," Mark added. "I'm around Joseph every day, but I never noticed he had shaved off his mustache."

Asaph became ash-white, drained of strength. Joseph was going to try to pass himself off as his twin brother, Zaanan!

That irrational boy! he thought as he entered his study. A message had been left on his table monitor: PHILIPPIANS 4:13. JOSEPH.

Ash-white

"I can do all things through Christ which strengtheneth me," Asaph quoted. "You're right, my boy — only a miracle of God can help you in this quest!"

Asaph decided to skip dinner, fast, and pray for Joseph, Allison, and Zaanan.

Praying for Joseph

Troz Space Colony

At that very moment, thousands of miles away on the backside of the moon, another orbiting space colony thrived: Troz, the largest of many rebel movements seeking world control.

The Sphere computer came to power after the nuclear Holocaust. Anyone who didn't agree with the Sphere's leadership and dominance was considered contaminated and very dangerous. This rebellion was commonly known as alien-thought, and was strictly forbidden.

Troz began as a movement not long after Sphere established its rule. The people of Troz were considered less civilized and more barbaric or primitive than those of Sphere. Through the years, the population of Troz had grown, to approximately five million. They were tribal in philosophy and encouraged to have as many children as possible. By Christian standards, their morals were tragically low.

Troz had secret outposts on earth, the moon's caverns, and various space stations. Though the Troz movement had always claimed a goal of destroying Sphere, it had never been much more than talk.

However, one day a man arose to challenge the leadership of Troz. He was a mysterious man who played on the superstitious nature of Troz's citizens. His name was Maroth, which is similar to the old Hebrew words meaning "bitter lordship." His use of theatrics and trickery made the people view him as almost supernatural. He only came out at certain times of his choosing and always wore a long, black, hooded robe. His hat was wide brimmed and pulled low on his brow. Only his angry, piercing eyes could be seen.

Maroth's reign of power had begun only a

Maroth

short time before, but already he had organized Troz into a force to be reckoned with. Troz's citizens had a long-standing disdain for computers and technology, preferring to fight and work with their hands and clubs. Maroth changed all that through a mixture of education and cruelty.

As if out of thin air, he provided weapons, spacecraft, information, and unity. This space station orbited opposite the revolution of the moon, so it always stayed hidden on the back side, away from earth. It had been established to build the Military Force Unification Project (MFUP), a giant flying robot with virtually indestructible armor. The unique part of this design was that each part of the robot was a separate military machine. From its head to its toes, the giant robot was a compilation of jets, land rovers, missile launchers, laser carts, and many other weapons. Shifts worked around the clock, feverishly trying to meet an impossible deadline.

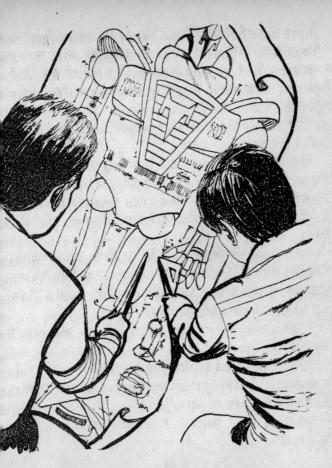

Military Force Unification Project

"We'll never make it," Larkin said. "We've only got a little over eleven days left, and we're nowhere close to completion. We haven't tested half the weapons, or even assembled the entire robot."

"Be careful, Larkin," warned his friend Kellner. "The air has ears."

The two men stood on a balcony overlooking a giant enclosed construction site. Thousands of people, looking more like ants, swarmed around a hundred or more various cars, planes, and the like.

"Most of these people don't even know what they're doing," observed the tired Larkin. "One simple mistake and this entire place could blow up like a fireworks display!"

"We must trust the judgment of Maroth," Kellner encouraged.

"Maroth! He hasn't even been here to see this monster!" Larkin retorted. "From where he sits, it's easy to give orders."

"Lower your voice," Kellner chided in a stern whisper.

"The air has ears"

"This monstrosity probably won't even get off the ground, and if it does, it will more than likely miss the city of Sphere and hit our people somewhere."

"This was mostly your project!"

"That's right. Done my way, on our timetable, anyone would have been defenseless against it," Larkin said.

"Listen, Larkin, you've been awake for two whole days. Why don't you go get some sleep? Things will look better to you if you do," Kellner pleaded.

"You're probably right. I believe I will get some sleep."

The two men left the balcony and went back inside a small area of upstairs offices. The space colony had been hastily erected just for the purpose of building this war machine. None of the walls, offices, or ceilings were finished; everything was rough.

Larkin went over to a makeshift cot covered in plans, books, and blueprints. The deafening

A makeshift cot

noise from the work area silenced as he closed the door behind him. He pushed everything off the cot, onto the floor, spilling paper and electronic gadgets all over the barren surface.

Kellner picked up some books and papers from a chair and neatly placed them on a mountain of clutter on Larkin's desk as Larkin lay down.

"Maybe if we . . ." began Kellner, only to stop when he looked over to see that Larkin was already fast asleep. He looked out through a giant observation window from his lofty perch. He could see welding and laser lights exploding in reflection on the work-area ceiling. He sat for a long time, staring at nothing. "Eleven days! Hah!" he laughed to himself.

"Eleven days! Hah!"

Ancient Paris

Zaanan sped in his new starjet across the Atlantic Ocean and landed in what once was Paris for refueling. After a few moments, he was back in flight.

He was amazed at the gadgetry his new starjet had. He locked his power arms into place on the armrests of his pilot seat, and the onboard computer extracted the new flight instructions from the power arm computer. Only enough information was given to get Zaanan from one destination to another, to be sure he wasn't followed.

Since this was the last portion of his journey, it

was time to review his assignment and his enemy's biographical profile. Up on a viewing screen, important data flashed.

"(CPGS) Citizens for a Planetary Globalized Society, the Planetarians, as they are called, are a relatively new group of terrorists who splintered off from Sphere, Troz, the Change Managers, and the Multicultural Futurists. They are believed to be small in number, highly secretive, and very advanced technologically."

A live action video of a man came on the screen. At the lower left portion of Zaanan's screen, a series of numbers and words flashed so fast that only his subconscious picked them up.

"This is Edolf, X2-TR3-51R. He was formerly a Sphere Imagineer," continued the narrator. "His primary function was to think. He defected three years ago and is the founder and leader of the CPGS."

Zaanan had learned most of this information during refresher courses on terrorist cults. Just as he was about to nod off from sheer boredom, the

EDOLF

X2-TR3-51R

BORN: FEBRUARY 9, 2962
BLOOD TYPE: "ø" NEGATIVE
BIRTH FUNCTION: COMPUTER IMAGINEER

CRIMINAL BIO -
DEFECTED: 3004 A.D.
ALIEN-THOUGHT: TERRORISM ESPIONAGE
CRIMES: ABDUCTED CITIZENS FROM SLEEP CENTER
FOUNDER: (CPGS) CITIZENS FOR A PLANETARY
          GLOBALIZED SOCIETY (PLANETARIANS)
LOCATION: NILE REGION SECTOR H-2
GOALS: UNKNOWN

lecture suddenly got interesting. A new face appeared on the starjet screen. Zaanan sat up and took renewed interest.

"Talgent Flara, P2-D9R-54, is your assisting agent. She is stationed in this region and is our most qualified expert on the Planetarians."

"Flame," said Zaanan in a voice just above a whisper. Zaanan hadn't seen Flame since their days at the Talgent Cadet School. Not long after Zaanan was commissioned, so was Talgent Flara, or Flame, as Zaanan called her.

She received her nickname because of her flaming red hair. She was as tough and intellectual as she was beautiful. Though they never had spoken of it, Zaanan felt that she had feelings for him, but the school was too difficult and strenuous, and no one wanted to jeopardize his future by becoming romantically involved. Openly, they were just good friends.

Zaanan had noted that she hadn't attended the recent award ceremony in his honor. He now felt

FLARA

P2-D9R-54

BORN: JULY 31, 2978
BLOOD TYPE: "A" NEGATIVE
BIRTH FUNCTION: MILITARY
COMMISSION: TALGENT WARRIOR
EXPERTISE: DESERT WARFARE
        PLANETARIAN TERRORISM
PRESENT ASSIGNMENT: NILE REGION
        SECTOR G-5
ALIEN-THOUGHT CONTAMINATION: NEGATIVE

happy to know that she had been stationed elsewhere and had not simply chosen to miss it.

The narrator continued to give information about where Zaanan was to meet Flame and more details of this assignment. Zaanan was now excited to be going to the land of the pyramids. He verbally ordered his ship to increase speed.

"Starjet 134-J, you are cleared for landing in Bay 1A," said Space Port Control. "Happy Holocaust Days to you."

"And the same to you," returned Zaanan. He laughed to himself how strange the words *happy* and *Holocaust* sounded together in the same greeting. He had heard it countless times before, without even noticing. Perhaps it was the heavy accent of the Space Port Controller.

Once again, Zaanan was somewhat amused about being directed to land in Bay 1A. Bay 1A was the only bay in the Space Port.

Zaanan climbed down from his starjet upon landing. Immediately a blast of desert heat

"Happy Holocaust Days to you"

struck his face. *Customs die hard,* he thought as he walked through the Space Port lobby. The lobby and the entire Space Port had Sphere architecture, but with old Egyptian design thrown in. As he exited the building, he squinted his eyes and wiped the fresh beads of sweat from his face and neck.

"This heat is unbelievable," he exclaimed to himself.

"If you don't like the weather, wait ten minutes. It will change," said a man squatting next to the wall of the Space Port, not looking up at Zaanan.

Zaanan thought he was joking until he noticed a heavy coat laying next to the man.

He checked the monitor on his power arms for a map that would lead him to Flame's meeting place. As he boarded the city transportation system monorail, he noticed the holiday decorations everywhere. They looked so festive and bright, but no one seemed to notice them. After

Outside the Space Port

five hundred years of celebrating Sphere's salvation of humanity, people were extremely weary. All the decorations were permanently mounted to buildings and home quarters. Near the holiday season, the city's central computer caused the decorations to come out of their wall storage areas in homes and buildings.

Prerecorded music flooded the streets with celebration; however, the people just walked on as if in a daze. Even Zaanan's loyalistic excitement was easily distracted by the thought of seeing Flame again. He got off the monorail in front of Sphere's headquarters. As he walked in, Flame walked out.

"Flame!" he yelled to his friend. "Wait for me!"

Flame didn't turn around, but she did slow down somewhat to let him catch up. "Hurry. I don't want to miss him," she said as Zaanan caught up with her.

The walkway areas in front of buildings began

"Flame! wait for me"

to fill up with emotionless people. Zaanan struggled to keep up with Flame as she pushed her way through the crowds.

A parade of sorts ambled down the street. Two floats hovered along, looking worn-out from years of use. Prerecorded music blared out, topping off the brief ceremony. As the floats moved on, so did the music.

Flame still hadn't looked at Zaanan. She kept checking her power arms for the location of her subject. "He's gone!"

"Who's gone?" Zaanan asked.

"Edolf! He was in our headquarters." She looked down at her feet and saw a small broken bugging device. "He found my tracer!" she said, picking up pieces of the shattered device. "We'll have to find him the hard way."

She turned to Zaanan and really acknowledged him for the first time.

"It's been a long time," he said.

"He found my Tracer"

"Yes, it has," Flame replied mater-of-factly. She was as beautiful as the last time he had seen her, but there was a difference in her eyes. She looked very tired and distant.

"It's good to see you again," Zaanan persisted.

"Snow is being predicted. We had better get prepared," she said, as if she hadn't heard Zaanan.

"Snow?"

Flame didn't reply to his question; she just walked back into Sphere Headquarters. Zaanan took note again of the Sphere Architecture with Egyptian design added in as he practically ran to keep up with her. She was heading for the accessory room for warm clothing. Zaanan finally caught up with her there. "What's wrong with you?" he asked.

She turned to him, planted her feet firmly, and poked him in the chest with a finger. "I told them I didn't need or want any help," she

"I don't want or need your help "

sneered. "I've been working on this case for a year, and I'm close to solving it, so stay out of my way."

Zaanan was stunned by her anger. He recalled, though, that her name was not only attributed to her hair color but also to her temper. Zaanan didn't want to argue, so he just tried to catch his snow gear as she threw it at him. At first he caught it, but his hands soon filled up, then his arms, his teeth, his knees — soon he was dodging clothing.

Flame looked over at him and saw the situation. She smiled, then chuckled, then broke into laughter that doubled her over. Zaanan dropped his equipment and joined her laughter. The tension between them had vanished.

"Za, I'm sorry I behaved as I did. It's just that I've been working night and day, trying to figure out this puzzle. I was angry when I heard they had assigned you here. I took it to mean that Sphere felt I wasn't carrying my weight."

Catching gear

"I don't think it's that way at all, Flame. The Planetarians stole three people from the Sleep Center, and I was sent to retrieve them. Our cases just happened to cross. I need your help, Flame."

"Now that you're here, I'm glad to see you."

They continued acquiring and loading their gear into a Desert Hawk, a traveling vehicle that flew close to the ground. As they flew out of headquarters, a rush of freezing wind slapped Zaanan in the face. Snow was falling quietly. He was amazed at the change in climate.

"I know that the weather is hard to forecast, but this is amazing!" he sighed.

"You should be closer to the Equator," Flame answered. "It's even more unpredictable there. The Holocaust must have affected the earth's revolution around the sun. A few more degrees, and this planet would have completely frozen or burned. Instead, we rock back and forth in these extreme weather patterns."

The Desert Hawk

"How long will this last?" Zaanan shouted as the wind picked up.

"Maybe ten minutes, maybe ten days. Who knows?"

As they left the city, the snow turned to a freezing drizzle. The Desert Hawk's doors and windows closed as they picked up speed.

"Where are the pyramids I've heard about?" Zaanan asked.

"Sphere destroyed them years ago. The Sphere didn't like their shape," Flame answered.

"Where are we really going?"

"You'll see."

They went west for many miles into the desert until they came to a small blockhouse. The freezing rain was snow again; the wind cut like a knife on any exposed flesh.

Flame knocked on the door, and a little round man answered. He ushered them inside his warm abode.

A little round man ushered them in

"How is she?" Flame asked as she took off her jacket.

"Close," answered the little man. His facial features and skin color reflected a long Egyptian heritage.

"Will you take us to her?"

"No. Absolutely not," the man refused. "Do I look as if I want to die?"

"What are you talking about?" Zaanan chimed in.

"We need you, Akheim," said Flame, ignoring Zaanan's question. "You're the only one who knows his way around her."

"No one knows his way around that volcano," replied Akheim. "One day a cave exists, the next it's gone, flooded with water or gushing lava. That volcano has many moods, and all of them are dark."

"Wait a minute! You're talking about a volcano in the middle of the desert?" Zaanan demanded.

"Do I look as if I want to die?"

"That's right!" Flame answered.

Suddenly Akheim heard a rustling noise outside.

"What's that?" Zaanan asked.

The blockhouse had no windows, so they couldn't look out.

"Someone's out there!" Akheim said with a husky voice.

All three burst out the front door to find a group of hooded people stripping the Desert Hawk.

"It's the Barrenites!" Akheim shouted as he fired a shot in the air with his laser blaster.

The Barrenites turned to look in their direction, then began to run away. Several were carrying field equipment belonging to Zaanan. Zaanan and Flame fired sonic waves, causing sand to blow up in every direction around the Barrenites, who dropped the equipment and ran off into the desert.

Once again the weather suddenly changed. The

The Barrenites

wind continued whipping along, herding the sand and clouds through the desert, but it was a warm, sunny wind.

Zaanan went out to retrieve a piece of equipment dropped by the Barrenites. When he turned around, he saw in the distance a giant volcano surrounded by a haze and thick black smoke that came from its crater. "Where did that come from?" he yelled back toward Flame. "I didn't see it when we got here!"

"The weather hid it from you," she answered.

At that moment, the earth shook. Zaanan, Flame, and Akheim instinctively fell to the ground, but as quickly as it had begun, the earthquake ended.

"It's getting close to erupting again, isn't it?" Flame asked.

"Yes, very close," Akheim admitted. "All the springs around this area have been getting hotter and hotter. The water has also been poisoned with volcanic salts and sulfur."

"Where did that come from?"

"We have less time than I thought," Flame said hurriedly. "Are you coming with us?"

"No," said Akheim. "I would just be in your way. I have nothing to give you. There are no maps, since new layers of lava flow constantly."

Flame and Zaanan got back into the Desert Hawk. Akheim hobbled over to them. "The Planetarians are in there. I'm sure of it," he said. "They are a dangerous people who fear nothing. Be very careful, my friends."

"Be careful my friends"

Pressing on

The Desert Hawk skimmed along on the desert's surface. The wind blew constantly, which was one reason the weather changed so much. Hot, black volcanic ash particles swirled around the desert.

Flame and Zaanan both wore protective goggles inside the Desert Hawk.

"Tell me about the Planetarians and why you think they're in the volcano," said Zaanan.

"Well," began Flame, "the Planetarians need the heat generated by an active Peléean volcano."

"Peléean?"

"Yes. That's the most violent type of volcano. This particular type has a hot magma capable of forging an alloy of magnesium and a new metal called Elementium. This combination, when fused, would create the most deadly weapon known to man. It would be easy to bring Sphere to its knees with this type bomb. Our sources tell us that they have capped off the conduit of the volcano."

"Conduit?" Zaanan was beginning to feel stupid.

"The neck or tunnel that the molten rock and gases rise to the surface through."

"Oh. I'm beginning to get the picture. They are at a point where they need help putting it all together. Edolf, being from Sphere, knew who could help him finish this last step, so he stole them from the Sleep Center."

"Now you're catching on," said Flame."

"There is one part that bothers me."

"What's that?"

"Well, one of the people taken was an athlete."

"They're creating the most deadly
weapon known to man"

"Maybe it was a mistake."

"Maybe," Zaanan said reluctantly.

They flew along for about two hours as the heat intensified outside the Desert Hawk.

"How do you plan to get in?" Zaanan asked, breaking the silence.

"Well, tunnels are often formed by flowing hot lava. When the lava flows, the outer surface hardens quickly on contact with air. The inner lava keeps on flowing, leaving a cave or tunnel where there had once been a molten river. A volcano can't be mapped because it is constantly producing more caves and closing others with lava. Sometimes, as in this case, the tunnels may be flooded."

"Water?"

"Yes, water," said Flame. "Water surrounds this volcano, making it like an island. Karmin, give me a diagram of this type of volcano," she instructed the computer. A diagram of the volcano filled the screen, and Flame pointed out to Zaanan the various layers and components of a volcano.

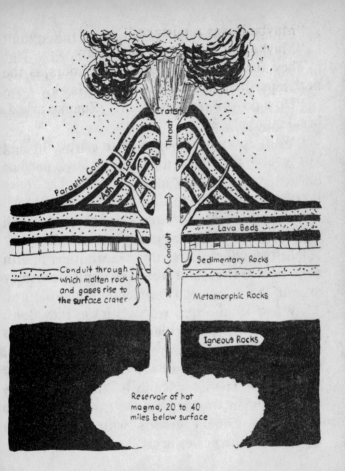

Peléean Volcano

"I think that they have capped off the conduit here at the lava-bed level," she explained. "This has added pressure and heat to the magma below. This pressure forces the volcano to form tunnels, or parasitic cones, on its side to release gases and lava."

"These are our openings for getting in and out, hopefully not getting caught, drowned, or burned," concluded Zaanan.

"Exactly."

"Since we have to cross this lake, what will keep us from being detected?" he asked.

"In two short years, this volcano has built a cone of two thousand feet. The common people around here feel it is somehow supernatural. They fear it and even worship it, so they don't expect anyone to try to enter it.

"Besides, only a genius or a crazy man would attempt what Edolf wants to do. Also, I feel that as unstable as this volcano is, they have every available man working on the cap site. We can fool their camera guards with the cloaking devices on our power arms."

"These are our openings"

"Either you're a smart woman, or this is all a nightmare," Zaanan said.

The Desert Hawk left land and soared across the lake surrounding the volcano. The closer they got to it, the fiercer the volcano looked. Red-hot molten lava oozed from the crater and ran down the cone on several sides. Great pieces of molten lava or volcanic bombs fired like cannons, scattering burning particles everywhere. Flame had to carefully maneuver the Desert Hawk away from falling debris.

"Cloaking device ready?" she asked.

"Ready!" Zaanan shouted as they got closer to the base of the volcano. Even inside the Desert Hawk, the heat from the volcano could be felt.

They landed without a welcoming committee present, so they assumed they had arrived unannounced. They put on protective gear consisting of oxygen helmets, heat-resistant clothing, and boots. Flame gave some last-minute instructions before they departed.

"You have only one hour of oxygen in your tank, so we have only one hour to get in, get our

"You have only one hour of oxygen."

people, and get out. Hopefully we're not too late.''

Zaanan was amazed at how well the suits fit and how easy it was to move around in them. They stepped out of the Desert Hawk and hot steam wrapped around his body. Zaanan felt dizzy and nauseous. They walked over to the base of the cone and surveyed the side. All at once a giant piece of molten lava fifteen feet around landed and rolled over the Desert Hawk, squashing it like a toy.

''Did the Desert Hawk figure into your plan of escape?'' Zaanan asked.

''Yes.'' She nodded slowly.

''What's your backup plan?''

''I have no other plan,'' she answered, turning back to the cone.

''What are the chances of Edolf actually capping off the volcano?'' Zaanan pressed.

''You ask too many questions!''

''Wait a second. I want to know what you think!''

No escape

"Edolf was a brilliant imagineer, but I didn't say he was an engineer!"

Suddenly the gravity of their situation dawned on Zaanan. He was attempting to stop a madman from trying to put a cork down the throat of an erupting volcano. Plus, their only means of escape at the moment was to swim across a lake of boiling water and lava.

Zaanan quickly signaled for Flame to take her helmet off. He was so insistent that she complied. Zaanan removed his and pulled her close in his arms. He kissed her, and to his surprise, she kissed him back.

A fresh rain of volcanic ash broke their embrace. They put their helmets back on and scanned the surface of the cone for an opening in the side. There were a few close to the bottom of the volcano, but they felt that those probably led down deep into the magma. About a hundred feet up, a steam cloud was billowing out of the side of the cone without any lava. They decided they would inspect it.

Kissing

Using their power arms, they flew up and found it to be an opening about five feet in diameter.

"This looks good to me. Let's try it," Zaanan suggested.

Oddly enough, inside the cavern, the heat wasn't as oppressive. The layers of hardened lava acted as insulation against the rising temperature. Also, most of the hot air was released through the crater of the volcano. They carefully walked down the tunnel, watching every direction.

The tunnel got smaller, and they had to crawl through. Seven minutes into the volcano, they came to a place where the cave split off in three different directions. They chose to follow the opening that had the greatest level of heat coming out. The farther they went into the side of the volcano, the darker and hotter it became. They used light wands from their power arms to light their pathway. Zaanan's countdown clock showed that they only had forty-three minutes of oxygen left in their tanks.

Inside the cavern

"Is it possible to stop the release of oxygen in this suit, once it starts?" he asked in a muffled voice.

"No."

The opening of the cave widened. The path showed wear from use.

"I believe we're onto something," Zaanan said.

"You're right," Flame agreed.

They slowed their pace and became more cautious when they saw an opening, getting down on their stomachs to crawl to the edge. Zaanan started to peer over when Flame stopped him. She signaled for him to watch her power arm, where a small, round mirror extended out on a telescoping rod and over the side.

Only a female Talgent would have makeup accessories as part of her power arms, thought Zaanan.

Flame was visibly pleased to see his surprise. Through the mirror they could see well enough to know that they could gaze over the side safely.

Talgent makeup mirror

They pulled themselves out to the edge for a better look.

They were only thirty feet above the cap site. The Planetarians' setup looked functional but crude. About ten people, male and female, worked busily below, checking levers and monitoring gauges. The three body tubes were no longer stacked, but they were still unopened. Edolf was there, working at a large computer console. Flame aimed her power arm camera at the monitor in front of Edolf and zoomed in.

That's why he was in Sphere headquarters! she thought to herself. *He was stealing the computer programs that show how to perform a mind probe on these people. He intends to wake them from their sleep, probe them, and discard them.*

She typed this information out on her power arm's minicomputer monitor and showed it to Zaanan. He had come to virtually the same conclusion.

Flame typed a question out on her minimonitor: "Do you have a plan?"

"Do you have a plan?"

"Yes," he said out loud as he began to craw
backward.

"What is it, then?"

"Let's give up," Zaanan said as he sat up an
raised his hands.

"Give up?" exclaimed Flame in a whispe
Then she turned around and saw the man stand
ing over Zaanan, pointing a large gun at h
head. Three other men stood behind the one wit
the gun.

Flame slowly raised her hands in surrende
The men had long, bushy hair and resembled a
cient cavemen. They didn't look very bright, b
they did have an equalizer.

They tied Zaanan's and Flame's hands behin
their backs, but didn't remove their power arm
As they marched single-file toward the cap sit
Zaanan rounded a curve in the cavern. Using h
power arms, he easily broke the bands on h
wrists. "Stun!" he yelled, voice activating h
power arms.

Before they knew what was happening, he r
leased an electric shock into three of the fo

"Let's give up"

captors. He turned in the fourth's direction just as the man fired his blaster. Zaanan jumped away just in time. The laser made a thunderous noise on impact, which echoed through the already loud volcano. Flame snapped her ropes and stunned their final captor from behind.

"We've got to work fast," Zaanan yelled as he ran past her toward the cap site. She fell in behind him.

Zaanan abruptly stopped, and she ran into him.

"Retreat!" he yelled.

She looked up and saw that the tunnel ahead was filled with what seemed to be an endless army of Planetarians. They both turned and ran the opposite direction. When they came to a fork in the caves, they went right instead of toward the surface. This move didn't throw the Planetarians off their trail in the least.

They took two other turns, but so did the Planetarians. They saw an opening ahead, so they ran toward it. They had worked their way back to the conduit of the volcano, but this time,

"Retreat!"

they were about three hundred feet above the cap site. It was hard to see down because of the black steam rising through the conduit of the volcano; however, Edolf seemed to be probing one of the people from the Sleep Center.

"What do we do now?" Flame yelled.

"Fly across the conduit to the other side," Zaanan ordered.

Flame switched her power arms to "flight mode" and flew the fifty yards across the conduit. Zaanan followed her. When he was about fifteen yards out, the Planetarians reached the opening he had just left and began firing their lasers at him. One blast hit his right power arm, killing its circuits. Now at half-power, he lost his ability to cross at the same angle, plowing into the side of the conduit and holding onto some jagged rocks.

Flame looked down from twenty-five feet above. She wanted to help Zaanan, but the Planetarians kept her pinned down with their lasers. She fired sonic blasts their way when

Flame flying

possible, to keep them from picking Zaanan off the wall.

The wall sloped inward, keeping Zaanan from getting a good foothold. He was just below another cave entrance, dangling almost three hundred feet above the magma of a volcano with one power arm shot and a group of cavemen taking target practice at him. He gritted his teeth and tried to pull himself upward, but couldn't.

Out of nowhere, a hand reached down and grabbed his arm. Zaanan looked up into the face of a giant man.

"Whose side are you on?" Zaanan asked with great difficulty.

"Neither," replied the man as two laser blasts hit near Zaanan's right ear.

"That's close enough, friend!" Zaanan yelled.

The man picked him up without any strain and set him down behind him. Suddenly a brilliant light flashed and a quaking sound shook the entire volcano. When Zaanan uncovered his eyes, the man was gone.

"Whose side are you on?"

The Planetarians retreated in haste, falling all over one another, while Flame moved to Zaanan's side.

"What *was* that?" she asked.

"An angel, I think!"

"A what?"

"Later," Zaanan said. "We've got to get out of here."

They ran down the cave, away from the conduit. Unexpectedly, Flame stopped. "What's that sound?" she asked.

"A volcano!"

"Not *that* sound. The other one. It sounds like water."

"Water?"

"Yes. Lava is porous. Sometimes it traps water in giant reservoirs. The quake from your 'angel' friend, added to the geothermal gradient, could produce enough pressure to release water — and the volcano, too!" she explained.

Just three feet ahead of them, the ceiling of the cave shifted, and hot water spewed out.

"You mean like that?" Zaanan asked.

Hot water spewing out

"Exactly," Flame screamed.

Zaanan took the lead and ran past her. She followed just as the ceiling burst wide open, letting loose a flood of water. They ran down the tunnel just ahead of the water.

"Where are we going?" Flame yelled as they ran.

"To the cap site," he replied, keeping up his pace.

"Shouldn't we try to get out?"

"The cap site is our only way out! Besides, I'm not leaving without the tubes."

"Forget the tubes!" she screamed as the water caught up with them.

"One tube contains my father!" he yelled back.

Though she felt stunned, the momentary disaster didn't allow time to stop and think. They ran past numerous Planetarians fleeing the volcano as rocks began to fall, water rushed in, and lava flowed. Steam spewed at every turn as they made their way to the cap site.

To the capsite

Edolf was alone, feverishly working to cap off the volcano. The giant circulator cap served as the floor for Edolf's laboratory and headquarters. The entire area was tossing like a ship on an angry sea.

Zaanan dashed over to an opened tube from the Sleep Center, checked the serial number on the side, and discovered it was not his father's tube. Water continued to gush in and flood the floor.

Edolf turned around and saw Zaanan and Flame, but was too busy trying to stabilize the volcano to react. Steam was beginning to shoot up from the edge of the cap as it rocked. A giant rumble from deep in the magma reservoir shook the colossal volcano's cone. Big rocks and molten ash fell everywhere.

"Help me get this tube over to the others," Zaanan yelled to Flame.

Without question, Flame pushed. The other two tubes were still attached to each other, so the two of them strained to get the third tube on top

Struggling

of the first two. The water continued to rush in and rise.

On a table near the tubes, Zaanan found the driver's saddle he'd seen the Planetarians use in the Sleep Center. He threw it over the top tube and strapped it on. "Get on!" he screamed to Flame, who immediately hopped on. "Edolf! Edolf! Come with us. It's too late to stop it."

Edolf looked up, then went back to his futile task. The hot water was now up to their waists.

"Let's go!" Flame yelled to Zaanan.

"I'm not leaving Edolf here," he countered, wading over to Edolf, who was banging on a valve with a wrench. Zaanan grabbed his shoulders. "It's over. Let's go!" he called.

Edolf whirled around and tried to hit Zaanan in the head with the wrench. Zaanan fell back and went underwater to avoid the blow, Edolf insanely went back to work.

Zaanan popped up out of the water and stunned Edolf with his power arm's stun gun, placed him over his shoulder, and waded through the hot water to the tubes, where he tossed him

Near miss

over the top tube on his stomach.

Zaanan positioned himself in the driver's seat and pressed the starter; the jet packs roared to life. The tube ship began to lift out of the rising water as pressure continued to mount on the cap site from deep below. The rumble grew and grew. Zaanan gave his makeshift ship full throttle, but their weight and ascending spiral pattern made the ship move slowly.

"Flame!" he shouted, "turn around and use your power arms. We need more lift."

Carefully but quickly, she turned and discharged every ounce of energy still left in her power arms into the "flight mode." The tube ship immediately picked up speed and altitude.

Zaanan noted that the walls were getting closer together. They were in the throat of the volcano. Black ash, fire, and smoke surrounded them as they climbed higher and higher.

Hundreds of feet below, the cap site could no longer withstand the pressure. The conduit of the volcano exploded with such force that the giant cap site was hurled with lightning speed toward

"We need more lift."

the surface. Just as the cap site struck the throat of the volcano, the tube ship cleared the crater and banked left. The cap site barely missed them as they sped toward land while the volcano erupted behind them.

When they were a safe distance away, they set the tube ship down on a flat area at the base of a mountain. Edolf was still unconscious when Flame tied him up.

"Is that your father?" Flame asked.

Zaanan was standing next to the tube ship. "According to this code number, 3TR-561-D, it is."

"What are you going to do?"

"Well, I'm not sure. If this date is correct," he said, pointing to a date on the side of the tube, "he wasn't supposed to be frozen for three more months, so he's probably just sleeping."

"Do you know how to bring him out of the sleep?"

"No. But I think I know someone who can."

"Are you taking him back to Sphere?" Flame asked.

Clearing the crater

Zaanan turned and faced her. "No, I'm not. I'm taking him to a safe place. Does that make sense to you?"

She walked over to a rock and leaned against it. "When I was a little girl," she began, "I used to lay awake at night and dream about my mother and father coming to get me. I know that our society teaches differently, but I still couldn't shake my desire to be with them. Yes, Zaanan, it makes sense."

"Then you won't report me?"

"I won't have to. You'll get caught."

"Sphere will never have to know that we got two people out," he said.

"That's right. The way I remember it, the Planetarians discarded two people. We were only able to bring one out."

Zaanan walked over to her, drew her close, and kissed her. When he stopped, he gazed deeply into her beautiful eyes. She reached up and kissed him.

"Talgent Flara," a voice said from her power arms. "Come in, Talgent Flara."

"I used to dream of my parents"

They broke off their embrace as if someone had walked up to them.

"Yes, this is Talgent Flara," she replied to her power arms.

"We will be at your location in five minutes."

"Thank you."

Flame gave them final directions to pick them up on the other side of the mountain. Quickly they scurried around and found a cave of sorts, where they hid Zaanan's father's tube before turning back to where they had left Edolf.

They helped the limp man to his feet.

In a few minutes, another Desert Hawk arrived. They strapped the remaining tube to the top and secured Edolf in the back.

The driver stood amazed as he watched the volcano continue to erupt and threaten. "I don't see how you got out of there in time!"

Zaanan climbed into the Desert Hawk behind Talgent Flara, they lifted off and began their journey to Sphere headquarters.

Flame leaned over to Zaanan and whispered,

Another Desert Hawk arriving

"Why did you call your friend in the volcano an angel?"

He smiled and said, "Later."

Their ride back to the Sphere base was uneventful, but anything would have been, compared to what they had gone through in the volcano.

Returning to base

Taking Edolf away

They arrived at headquarters near noon.

"I am totally exhausted," admitted Flame as they got out of the Desert Hawk.

Sphere guards came and took Edolf and the tube away.

"I'm going to go report and then sleep for a month," Flame volunteered. "What about you?"

"I believe I'll go get my starjet and take one last look at the volcano before heading back."

"I figured you would say that," Flame said with a smile. "Leave your broken power arm here and I'll have it fixed and sent to you. Who knows, now that my assignment is finished here, I just might bring it to you in person."

Zaanan resisted the urge to kiss her again. No sense in arousing suspicion. "I'd like that. I'd like that very much," he replied.

He turned and walked away, heading for the Space Port to get his starjet. When he reached the corner, he turned to see if she was still there. She wasn't. He had wanted to thank her for keeping his secret.

It was late afternoon when he arrived at the place they had hidden his father's tube. Zaanan carefully mounted it inside his starjet, then walked up the mountain to the edge of a plateau. The volcano wasn't nearly as angry as it had been a few hours before. The sun was beginning to set, and the crater glowed a fluorescent yellow and magenta.

As usual, the weather was changing. The wind had died down, and the earth was cooling off. As Zaanan stood on the plateau, a fog began to fill

Deep in thought

the valley below. The vapor mist inched up as Zaanan stood perfectly still, deep in thought.

He wondered about himself. His plan, as foolish as it sounded, was to get his father to Asaph in the Fatal Limit. He hoped the Christians could help revive him.

Where would he find his mother? He stood there dreaming of them all being together somehow, someday. The fog began to gently curl around his ankles. He turned and walked down from the plateau to his starjet. The fog parted just enough to let him pass through, then it silently closed up and settled, as if he had never been there. It was as if nature somehow knew his plan and wanted to shield him from the danger and risk and terror and peril he would face in the coming days.

His starjet roared to life and took off in search of the Fatal Limit and another adventure.

. . . To be continued!

Will the Christians in the Fatal Limit revive Zaanan's father?

Will Zaanan's twin brother, Joseph, save Allison from prison?

Will the giant robot destroy Sphere in eleven days?

Will Zaanan become a Christian?

For these answers and more, read the next exiting episode of Zaanan.

"The Ransom of Renaissance"
in
YOUNG READER'S CHRISTIAN LIBRARY

219